This
Harry and the
Dinosaurs
book belongs to

· · · · · · · · · · · · · · · · · · · · · ·

# SCELIDOSAURUS

(ske-LI-doh-SAW-rus)

# TYRANNOSAURUS

(tie-RAN-oh-SAW-rus)

# TRICERATOPS

(try-SER-a-tops)

# STEGOSAURUS

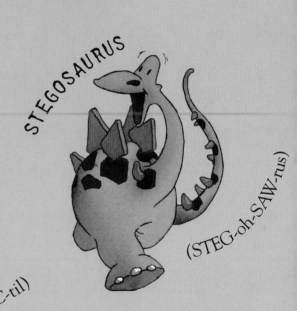

(STEG-oh-SAW-rus)

# PTERODACTYL

(TER-oh-DAC-til)

# APATOSAURUS

(a-PAT-oh-SAW-rus)

# ANCHISAURUS

(AN-ki-SAW-rus)

SCELIDOSAURUS

(ske-LI-doh-SAW-rus)

TYRANNOSAURUS

(tie-RAN-oh-SAW-rus)

TRICERATOPS

(try-SER-a-tops)

STEGOSAURUS

(STEG-oh-SAW-rus)

PTERODACTYL

(TER-oh-DAC-til)

APATOSAURUS

ANCHISAURUS

(AN-ki-SAW-rus)

(a-PAT-oh-SAW-rus)

With love to Teddy, Amelie, Ella and Sophia,
my dream team! – I.W.

For Karl Garrill,
Cambridge United's staunchest supporter – A.R.

PUFFIN BOOKS

UK | USA | Canada | Ireland | Australia
India | New Zealand | South Africa

Puffin Books is part of the Penguin Random House group of companies
whose addresses can be found at global.penguinrandomhouse.com.

www.penguin.co.uk   www.puffin.co.uk   www.ladybird.co.uk

Penguin
Random House
UK

First published 2009
This edition published 2016
001

Text copyright © Ian Whybrow, 2009
Illustrations copyright © Adrian Reynolds, 2009
All rights reserved
The moral right of the author and illustrator has been asserted

Made and printed in China

ISBN: 978-0-141-37506-9

All correspondence to:
Puffin Books
Penguin Random House Children's
80 Strand, London WC2R 0RL

# Harry and the Dinosaurs United

Ian Whybrow  Adrian Reynolds

PUFFIN

It was nearly time for the school football competition, and Harry had been picked as captain for his class team.

"Hands up who wants to be in Harry's team?" asked Mrs Rance.

All the dinosaurs put up their feet,
so Harry picked them first.

Next he picked Jack and Charlie, Mia
and Muhammad. They were going to play
Scarlett's team from Mr Jackson's class.

At break time, Harry and the dinosaurs
discussed positions.

Triceratops and Tyrannosaurus said,
"Raaah! Can we both be goalie?"
and Harry said yes, why not.
    Pterodactyl said, "Can I be wingie?"
    "Definitely!" said Harry.

After school, Harry and his team went to
Mr Oakley's field to practise.

Everyone enjoyed chasing about,
but they kept getting in each other's way.
  Then Sam turned up.
  "Right. All of you against just me . . . OK?"

They all ran after Sam, but no way could they catch her. And when they were all puffed out she dodged past them and scored.

"Raaaah! Not fair! Too quick!" said the dinosaurs.

"Anybody can beat you lot!" shouted Sam. "You're useless!"

Sam did her celebration skid.
That was why Harry kicked the ball over
the hedge for Mr Oakley's dog Morgan to chase.

Mr Oakley and Nan heard all the shouting
and came to settle things down.

"You don't boot balls to Morgan if you don't want them busted!" Mr Oakley said to Harry.

"Yes, but Sam says we're useless," Harry complained.

"Don't talk daft!" said Nan. "You just need more practice, that's all."

"Teamwork! That's what you need," said Mr Oakley. "Tell you what, why don't you come back tomorrow and give us oldies a game?"

Next day, old Tom Powell from down the lane
turned up with Trevor from the shop
and Gary the postman.
    The dinosaurs were a bit worried
about playing; they didn't want to be useless.
    "Is this dribbling?" said Stegosaurus.
    Harry said yes, but the wrong sort.

"Raaaah! On my head!" roared Triceratops.
He tried heading bubbles, but it was no good;
they kept going pop!
Harry said, "Don't worry, my dinosaurs.
You can be our *mascotauruses*!"

While Mr Oakley's team warmed up,
Jack taught Charlie back-heeling and
Muhammad showed Mia step-overs.

But Harry knew the best trick of all . . .
working together as a team.

"Don't everybody chase after the ball," he said.
"Stay in position or run into a space
and call for a pass."

On the day of the competition,
Harry and the dinosaurs were nervous.

The kids in Scarlett's team were BIG.
They could all do keepie-uppies,
and they had proper kit with numbers
and everything.

But Nan had made some special shirts
for Harry's team.

"Heads up and do your best!
Remember we're a team," said Harry.
"Now hold on to your mascotauruses
and let's go!"
    "RAAAAH!" roared Dinosaurs United.

Scarlett's side started well,
and by half-time they were winning two–nil.

"Come on," encouraged Harry.
"Play together and we can beat them!"

And all the mascotauruses roared:
"Ooo-ahhh!
Give us a RAAAAH!"

After the break, Harry's side played just like
a real football team.
They stayed in position and moved the ball quickly.
And, with just two minutes to go,
they equalized . . . two all!

All the fans really got behind them, chanting:
        "Di-nos
        U-ni-ted
        Can ne-ver be di-vi-ded!"
    Harry ran as fast as he could.
    He made some space.
            He called for the ball.
                "Pass it, Jacko!"
                    Nothing fancy . . .
                        Side-foot . . .

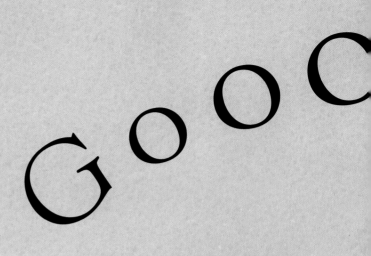

GoOO

The crowd cheered, the dinosaurs cheered;
Dinosaurs United were the winners!
    "RAAAAH!"

On the way home, Mr Oakley said to Nan,
"You can't beat us old Dinosaurs, eh?"
    "Not when we play as a team!" said Harry.
    "RAAAAH!" said Dinosaurs United.

ENDOSAURUS

SCELIDOSAURUS

(ske-LI-doh-SAW-rus)

TYRANNOSAURUS

(tie-RAN-oh-SAW-rus)

TRICERATOPS

(try-SER-a-tops)

STEGOSAURUS

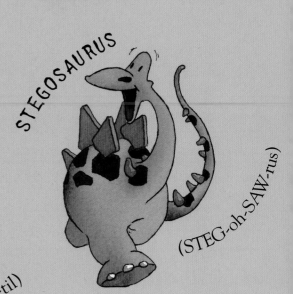

(STEG-oh-SAW-rus)

PTERODACTYL

(TER-oh-DAC-til)

APATOSAURUS

(a-PAT-oh-SAW-rus)

ANCHISAURUS

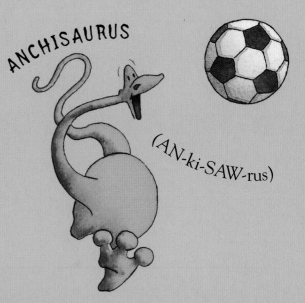

(AN-ki-SAW-rus)

## SCELIDOSAURUS

(ske-LI-doh-SAW-rus)

## TYRANNOSAURUS

(tie-RAN-oh-SAW-rus)

## TRICERATOPS

(try-SER-a-tops)

## PTERODACTYL

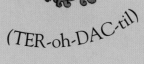

(TER-oh-DAC-til)

## STEGOSAURUS

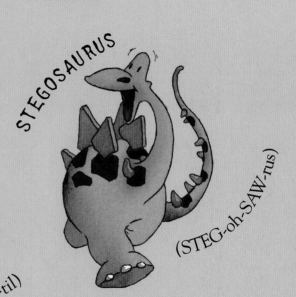

(STEG-oh-SAW-rus)

## APATOSAURUS

(a-PAT-oh-SAW-rus)

## ANCHISAURUS

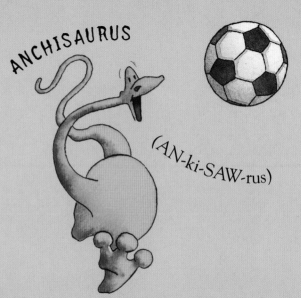

(AN-ki-SAW-rus)